BOOK CLUB EDITION

The Bears'
PICNIC

by Stan and Jan Berenstain

BEGINNER BOOKS   A Division of Random House, Inc.

This title was originally catalogued by the Library of Congress as follows: Berenstain, Stanley. The bears' picnic, by Stan and Jan Berenstain. [New York] Beginner Books [1966] 56 p. col. illus. 24 cm. "B-41." I. Berenstain, Janice, joint author. II. Title. PZ7.B4483Be 66—9210 ISBN: 0-394-80041-9 ISBN: 0-394-90041-3 (lib. bdg.)

D   9 0

The Bears'

PICNIC

Mother Bear,
put your apron away.
We are going to go
on a picnic today!

Where are we going
on our picnic, Dad?

To the very best place
in the world, my lad!

Now you remember
this spot, my dear.
When we were young,
we picnicked here.

Papa, I do not
like to complain,
but your wonderful spot
is next to a train!

Where are we going
now, Papa Bear?
Is there another
wonderful spot somewhere?

Don't pester me
with questions, please.
There's a place I know
right in those trees.

It is everything
a picnic spot should be.
And no one remembers
it is here but me.

What a spot! What a spot!
So quiet! So cool!
Just as it was
when I was in school.

We had a school picnic
and I won first place
for eating the most pie
in a pie-eating race.

Pop, this spot may
be very fine,
but look what it says
on that big sign!

Dad,
can you find us
another spot?
Are we having
a picnic
today, or not?

Now stop asking questions!
Be quiet! Stop stewing!
Your father knows
what he is doing.

To pick a spot that is
just the right one,
you have to be very
choosy, my son.

Nothing can bother
our picnic here!
Lay out the picnic
things, my dear.

I do not like
to say so, Dad,
but another good spot
has just gone bad.

I hope there's another
good spot you know.
But how much farther
do we have to go?

Why don't you use
your eyes, Small Bear?
There's a perfect place
right over there!

The grass is green.
The air is sweet.
Lay out the lunch,
and take a seat.

Hooray!
At last
we're going to eat!

Well . . .

this place is good.

I wasn't wrong.

But I know one better.

Let's move along.

Now take this perfect
piece of ground.
No one but us
for miles around!

Pop, you picked
the best spot yet.
But how can we picnic
with that jet?

I am very
hungry, Pop!
When is this spot-picking
going to stop?

I am getting tired.
My feet hurt, too.
Any old spot here
ought to do.

Please, Pop, please,
can't we picnic soon?
It's long past lunch.
It's afternoon!

You have to be choosy,
Pop, I know.
But what's better up here
than down below?

What's up here? ...
I'll tell you what.
The world's most perfect
picnic spot!

As you can see,
it is perfectly clear
that *nothing* can bother
our picnic here.

No noisy crowds!

No pesky planes!

And no mosquitoes,

trucks or trains!

Oh-oh, Dad.

Here come the rains!

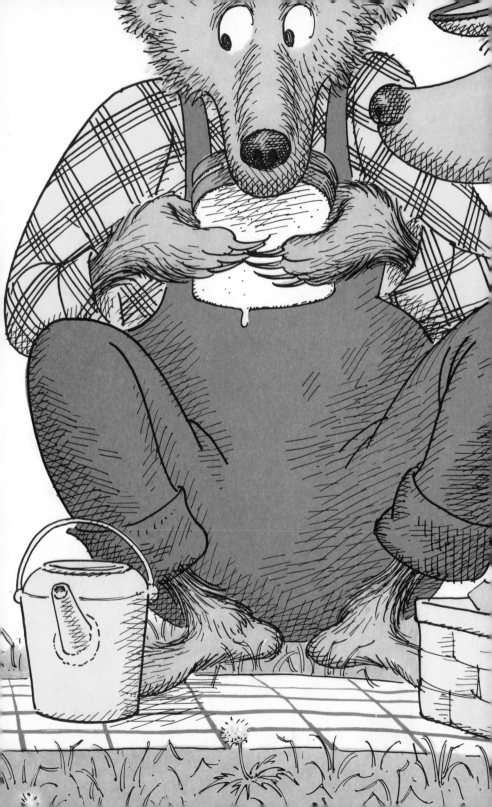

Pooh!
Rain to a bear
is nothing at all.
We'll picnic here
and let it fall.

Come back!

What kind of bears are you?

Scared of a drop

of rain or two!

Bring back that food!

This place will do.

It's dry in here.

It's warm here, too!

It does look warm.

Yes, I agree.

But it looks much, much
too warm for me!

Wait, now! Wait!
You wait for me!
I'll find a better spot.
You'll see.

I'll find the perfect
place to eat.
I'll find a spot
that can't be beat!
The finest spot
you've ever seen....

Now,
THAT
is the kind
of place I mean!

He did it,
Mother.
Did he not?
He found the perfect
picnic spot!